A Caring Neighbour

Karema Bouroubi

The Islamic Foundation

*Dedicated to all the children
of the Abu Bakr Islamic School,
Cambridge, UK*

MUSLIM CHILDREN'S LIBRARY

General Editors: **M. Manazir Ahsan** and **Anwar Cara**

A CARING NEIGHBOUR

Author: **Karema Bouroubi**
Illustrations: **Lubna Hoque**

Published by
The Islamic Foundation, Markfield Dawah Centre,
Ratby Lane, Markfield, Leicestershire LE67 9RN, UK

Quran House, PO Box 30611, Nairobi, Kenya

PMB 3193, Kano, Nigeria

MUSLIM CHILDREN'S LIBRARY

An Introduction

Here is a new series of books, but with a difference, for children of all ages. Published by the Islamic Foundation, the Muslim Children's Library has been produced to provide young people with something they cannot perhaps find anywhere else.

Most of today's children's books aim only to entertain and inform or to teach some necessary skills, but not to develop the inner and moral resources. Entertainment and skills by themselves impart nothing of value to life unless a child is also helped to discover deeper meaning in himself and the world around him. Yet there is no place in them for God, Who alone gives meaning to life and the universe, nor for the divine guidance brought by His prophets, following which can alone ensure an integrated development of the total personality.

Such books, in fact, rob young people of access to true knowledge. They give them no unchanging standards of right and wrong, nor any incentives to live by what is right and refrain from what is wrong. The result is that all too often the young enter adult life in a state of social alienation and bewilderment, unable to cope with the seemingly unlimited choices of the world around them. The situation is especially devastating for the Muslim child as he may grow up cut off from his culture and values.

The Muslim Children's Library aspires to remedy this deficiency by showing children the deeper meaning of life and the world around them; by pointing them along paths leading to an integrated development of all aspects of their personality; by helping to give them the capacity to cope with the complexities of their world, both personal and social; by opening vistas into a world extending far beyond this life; and, to a Muslim child especially, by providing a fresh and strong faith, a dynamic commitment, an indelible sense of identity, a throbbing yearning and an urge to struggle, all rooted in Islam. The books aim to help a child anchor his development on the rock of divine guidance, and to understand himself and relate to himself and others in just and meaningful ways. They relate directly to his soul and intellect, to his emotions and imagination, to his motives and desires, to his anxieties and hopes - indeed, to every aspect of his fragile, but potentially rich personality. At the same time it is recognized that for a book to hold a child's attention, he must enjoy reading it; it should therefore arouse his curiosity and entertain him as well. The style, the language, the illustrations and the production of the books are all geared to this goal. They provide moral education, but not through sermons or ethical abstractions.

Although these books are based entirely on Islamic teachings and the vast Muslim heritage, they should be of equal interest and value to all children, whatever their country or creed; for Islam is a universal religion, the natural path.

We invite parents and teachers to use these books in homes and classrooms, at breakfast tables and bedsides and encourage children to derive maximum benefit from them. At the same time their greatly valued observations and suggestions are highly welcome.

To the young reader we say: You hold in your hands books which may be entirely different from those you have been reading till now, but we sincerely hope you will enjoy them; try, through these books, to understand yourself, your life, your experiences and the universe around you. They will open before your eyes new paths and models in life that you will be curious to explore and find exciting and rewarding to follow. May God be with you forever.

We are grateful to everyone who has helped in the publication of this book, particularly Dr. A.R. Kidwai, Br. Anwar Cara and Dr. A. Siddiqui who read the manuscript with great interest and offered valuable suggestions.

May Allah bless with His mercy and acceptance our humble contribution to the urgent and gigantic task of producing books for a new generation of children, a task which we have undertaken in all humility and hope.

September 1996   **M. Manazir Ahsan**
Rabī' al-Thānī 1417   **Director General**

Guide to Pronouncing Arabic Words

For some Arabic vowels and sounds there is no English equivalent. In order to help the readers overcome this problem some special marks have been put on certain words in this book.

For example, ā, ī and ū stand for the vowel sounds aa (as in path), ii (as in feet) and oo (as in pool) respectively.

Similarly, the signs (') and (') have been used for the Arabic letters 'hamza' (as in Insha' Allah) and 'ayn' (as in 'Id).

Mrs Ahmad, who lived next door to Nazia in Appletree Drive, was suddenly taken ill. She was rushed to hospital in an ambulance. It was Nazia, while playing with her friends Hannah, Yacine and Nahla, who had seen poor Mrs Ahmad fall to the ground.

Being a sensible and thoughtful girl, she immediately ran to raise the alarm. Nazia's mother telephoned Mr Ahmad at his place of work to tell him what had happened. He rushed to the hospital to be at his wife's side.

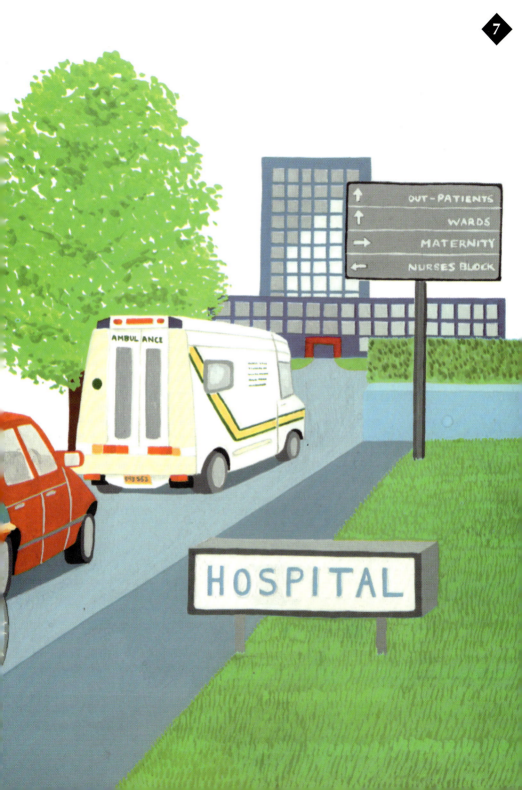

In the confusion, Mr Ahmad and Nazia's mother had forgotten all about little Yasmin and Amel, the twin daughters of Mr and Mrs Ahmad, who were still next door.

'There's nobody to look after Yasmin and Amel', said Nazia fearfully.

'Don't worry Nazia' replied her mother, 'we'll be good neighbours and do our duty as Muslims. We will look after them until their mummy is well again *Inshā' Allāh*. Now be a good girl and go next door and fetch them, they must be frightened, poor little dears.'

Nazia quickly went round to Mr and Mrs Ahmad's house. She found the twins sitting on the bottom step of the stairs, their arms wrapped tightly around each other.

'Come on you two', laughed Nazia, 'come to our house, my mum will look after you.' Nazia looked down at the twin's unhappy faces and bent down to pick them up. 'Don't worry! *Inshā' Allāh* your mummy will get better and be able to come home soon.' Nazia took the twins back to her house, and decided she would take care of them.

She would let them play with her toys and would read them a story. She was sure they would enjoy that and it would help them to forget the reason for their sadness, *Inshā' Allāh*.

Nazia took them to her bedroom and showed them all the exciting toys and told them, 'You can play with whatever you like.'

Yasmin and Amel looked eagerly around the room. They could not decide what to play with first.

Nazia watched them thoughtfully; she was thinking of how fortunate she herself was. She had parents who loved her a lot and were very generous to her. She silently thanked Allah for giving her such a wonderful mother and father.

The twins must really miss their mummy, thought Nazia. She felt sad and said a little prayer, asking Allah to restore Mrs Ahmad to good health.

Nazia then went downstairs to help her mother. She entered the kitchen where her mother was speaking on the telephone.

Her mother was telephoning the hospital about visiting hours. She hung up the phone and turned to face Nazia. 'Oh! I didn't hear you come in', she exclaimed. 'That was the hospital! We can go and visit Mrs Ahmad after lunch, *Inshā' Allāh.'*

'Oh, brilliant!' yelled Nazia, excitedly running from the kitchen, completely forgetting that she had come to offer to help her mother.

Nazia burst through the bedroom door, making Yasmin jump in surprise. 'We are going to see your mum after lunch', gushed Nazia happily. The twins jumped up and started leaping about the room, cheering and shouting excitedly.

They all ran downstairs and scampered through to the kitchen. Nazia's mother was busy preparing lunch for them all and something special to take to the hospital for Mrs Ahmad. She knew that Mrs Ahmad would not want to eat hospital food, because it might contain some ingredients which are forbidden to Muslims.

'What are you doing mummy?' asked Nazia.

'I am preparing a meal for Mrs Ahmad', replied her mother.

'Why?' asked Nazia. 'Doesn't the hospital have any food?'

'Of course they do', laughed her mother, 'but it is required of all good Muslims to visit the sick and it is good to take some food for them.'

'Oh! I think I had better make something too then', said a rather worried Nazia. 'I want to be a good Muslim.'

'Don't worry about making something, you can buy a gift at the local shop, *Inshā' Allāh*', answered her mother.

After lunch, Nazia helped her mother to clear away the dishes. She was determined to be good to her mother. Her father was always telling her the famous ḥadīth 'Paradise lies at the feet of your mother.'

He told her that if she was always respectful and kind to her mother, she would, *Inshā' Allāh*', go to Paradise.

When she had finished the dishes, Nazia went to get the twins ready. She put their shoes and coats on and then got ready herself. Then they all set out for the hospital. They went to the corner shop before going to catch the bus.

'What would you like to buy for Mrs Ahmad children?' asked Nazia's mother.

'We want to buy chocolates, grapes, and a book for Mrs Ahmad to read', answered Nazia on behalf of everyone.

When they arrived at the bus-stop, they checked the timetable to see how long they would have to wait for the bus. Yasmin and Amel were getting impatient and kept asking to see their mother.

'Ah! Here comes the bus, *alḥamdulillāh*', said Nazia's mother with a sigh of relief.

They all clambered aboard. 'Hurray', cheered the twins, 'we're on our way!'

The hospital was very busy. They followed the signs to the ward.

As they entered the ward, they saw Mrs Ahmad sitting up in bed at the far end of the ward. As soon as Yasmin and Amel saw their mother, they squealed with delight, raced across the ward and jumped into their mother's open arms. Nazia and her mother sauntered over slowly, giving the twins some time alone with their mother.

'*Assalāmu 'Alaikum*', said Nazia and her mother.

'*Wa-'Alaikum as-Salām*', answered Mrs Ahmad. 'Thank you for coming and bringing my daughters to see me. May Allah reward you for this kindness.'

'It's my pleasure,' replied Nazia's mother.

'How are you feeling?'

'*Alḥamdulillāh*, not too bad,' said Mrs Ahmad. 'Maybe just a little tired.'

Nazia gave Mrs Ahmad the food her mother had cooked.

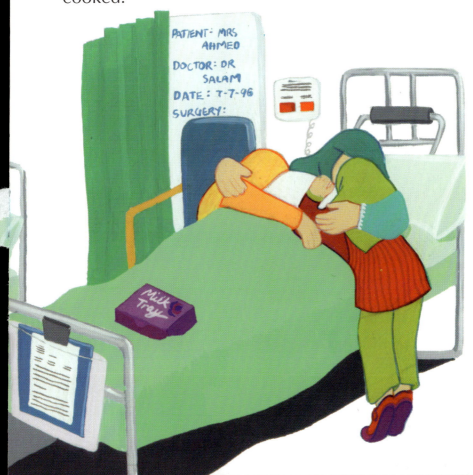

'Oh, lovely! *Jazākallāh khairan*', smiled Mrs Ahmad. 'You are very helpful and kind *Māshā' Allāh.*'

'It's nothing! If we do not care for one another, who else will care for us', said Nazia's mother.

Soon it was time to leave. It had been decided that the twins would stay at Nazia's house that night. When they got home, Nazia made a drink for everyone. She then took Yasmin and Amel out to the garden to play. They had cried all the way home and she wanted to cheer them up.

Nazia's mother went to the bathroom to perform *wuḍū'*. It was time for *'Asr* prayer. When she had finished her prayers, she said a special prayer for Mrs Ahmad, asking Allah to give her good health.

After dinner, Nazia asked her mother to read a selection of *ḥadīth*. 'They may bring comfort to Yasmin and Amel's mummy', said Nazia.

They seated themselves comfortably on the floor and Nazia's mother read them some *ḥadīth* about visiting the sick and how to treat neighbours.

'By Allah, he has no faith whose neighbours are not safe from his wickedness.' 'Allah is not kind to him who is not kind to people.' 'Visit the sick, feed the hungry and free the slaves.'

'So we must remember to be kind to one another and visit the sick, these are some of the basic virtues of Muslims', said Nazia's mother. 'Think of the Holy Qur'ān and the *sunnah* of the Prophet Muḥammad as a guide which we use to find the right path. Read it carefully and follow it and, *Inshā' Allāh,* you will never get lost.'

The next morning, Nazia's mother phoned the hospital to inquire about Mrs Ahmad. 'Oh! She's fine. She will be released this afternoon', said the nurse cheerfully. Nazia's mother rushed upstairs to wake the children and give them the good news. 'Your mummy's coming home today.' They leapt out of bed and ran over to her, hugged her tightly and shouted: 'Thank you! Thank you!' Nazia and her mother smiled happily at Yasmin and Amel's excitement.

Both of their prayers had been answered and Mrs Ahmad would soon be home and in good health, *alḥamdulillāh.* The twins would have their mother back and everything would be as it was before Mrs Ahmad was taken ill, *Inshā' Allāh.*

Glossary of Islamic Terms

Alḥamdulillāh	Praise be to God (Allah).
'Asr prayer	Afternoon prayer.
Assalāmu 'Alaikum	Peace be with you.
Ḥadīth	Sayings of the Prophet Muḥammad (peace be upon him).
Inshā' Allāh	If God is willing.
Jazākallāh khairan	May God reward you better.
Māshā' Allāh	Whatever may be the will of God.
Qur'ān	The Muslims' Holy book.
Sunnah	Example of the Prophet Muḥammad's life.
Wa-'Alaikum as-Salām	And peace be with you too.
Wuḍū'	Ablution or cleansing of parts of the body performed by Muslims before starting their prayers.